This Ladybird book

belongs to

J|1932272

A catalogue record for this book is available from the British Library

Published by Ladybird Books Ltd
27 Wrights Lane London W8 5TZ
A Penguin Company

2 4 6 8 10 9 7 5 3 1

Printed in Italy

Here
comes
Dad

by Irene Yates
illustrated by Nicola Evans

Ladybird

Here comes Dad, he's ready to play.
What do you think he is today?

Dad is a troll – a tremendous,
trundling troll!

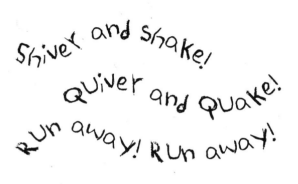

Shiver and shake!
Quiver and quake!
Run away! Run away!

"I'm a troll, a trundling troll!

waaaah!"

Here comes Dad, he's ready to play.
What do you think he is today?

Dad is a monster – a massive,
magnificent monster!

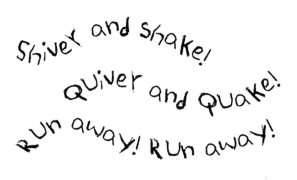

Shiver and shake!
Quiver and Quake!
Run away! Run away!

"I'm a monster, a massive monster!

Growwwl..."

Here comes Dad, he's ready to play.
What do you think he is today?

Dad is a crocodile – a creeping,
crawling crocodile!

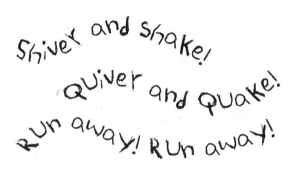

Shiver and shake!
Quiver and quake!
Run away! Run away!

"I'm a croc, a creeping croc!

Snip! Snap!"

Here comes Dad, he's ready to play.
What do you think he is today?

He's a giant – a juddering,
gigantic giant!

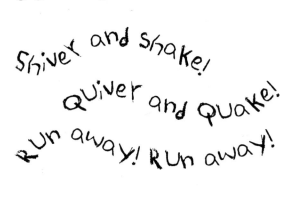

Shiver and shake!
Quiver and quake!
Run away! Run away!

"I'm a giant, a gigantic giant!

Grrrrr..."

Here comes Dad, he's ready to play.
What do you think he is today?

He's a snake – a slithery,
slathery snake!

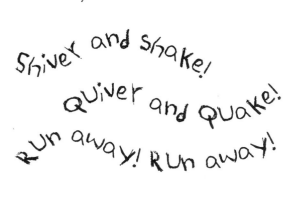

Shiver and shake!
Quiver and quake!
Run away! Run away!

"I'm a snake, a slithery snake!

HiSSSSS..."

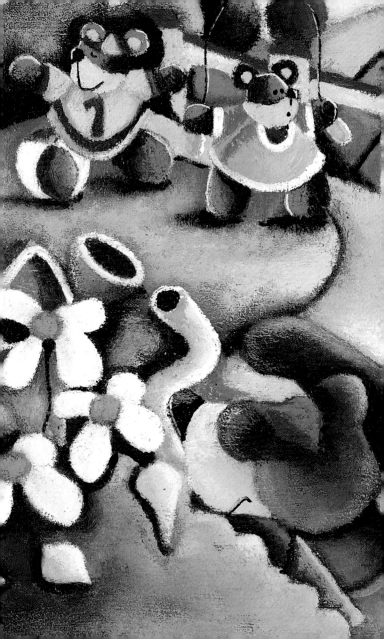

Here comes Dad, he's ready to play.
What do you think he is today?

He's a lion – a loping,
lolloping lion!

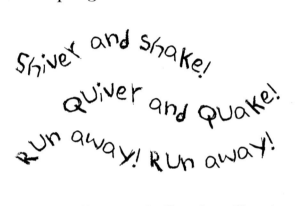

Shiver and shake!
Quiver and Quake!
Run away! Run away!

"I'm a lion, a lolloping lion!

RoaR..."

Here comes Dad, he's ready to play.
What do you think he is today?

Is he a **troll**?

Is he a **monster**?

Is he a **crocodile**?

Is he a **giant**?

Is he a **snake**?

Is he a **lion**?...

…no, he's just Dad.

Lovely, lovely Dad.
Reading us stories, hugging
us tight, keeping us safe
all day and all night!